Enid Blyton's
NODDY
and his New Friend

BBC BOOKS

It had been a quiet day in Toyland. Noddy was feeling rather bored and was looking for something exciting to do.

As he drove into town, he found that Mr Plod had blocked the street with a line of traffic cones.

"I put these here," said Mr Plod, pointing to the cones, "so I could direct all the caravans from Binks' circus around the town."

"A *circus*!" cried Noddy. "That's exciting. May I follow it?"

"If you must," said Mr Plod, and before he could change his mind, Noddy drove straight through the cones, sending them skidding across the street.

Further along the road, Noddy came across
a funny-looking creature, sitting under a tree,
moaning and clutching his foot.

"What *are* you?" asked Noddy. "Do you belong
in the circus?"

"I am a Bunkey," said the strange animal. "Half a monkey and half a rabbit. Can't you see my rabbit ears? I fell off a circus caravan and hurt my leg. Ow! . . ."

"Well, I could drive after the circus and help you back into your caravan," said Noddy.

"Oh, no, I don't want to go back to the circus, *please*!" cried the Bunkey. "They were horrid to me!"

"Poor Bunkey," said Noddy. "You can stay at my house until your leg's better."

"Oh, thank you," said the Bunkey gratefully.

He climbed into Noddy's car, and they drove back at top speed into Toy Town, almost knocking poor Mr Plod over on the way.

Back at Noddy's house, Noddy and the Bunkey
were enjoying a cup of cocoa together.

"I do like your house, Noddy," said the Bunkey.
"I shall sleep in this cosy chair and when my *leg*'s
better, I'll clean your house from top to bottom,
cook your dinner, wash and polish your car,
weed your garden, do your shopping . . ."

"Good gracious!" said Noddy. "You need not do all that!"

"Oh, please!" said the Bunkey. "I want to repay your kindness!"

"All right then, if you really want to," said Noddy.

...od as his word, the Bunkey cleaned and polished
...dy's car until it shone.

"...ve never seen my car gleam like that, Bunkey!"
...d Noddy. "Thank you."

...When Tessie Bear came to ask Noddy if he would drive
...er into town, Noddy introduced her to his new friend.

"Noddy has been so kind to me," said the Bunkey, "that I really want to help him, and if you are his friend, then I want to help you too. Whenever you want anything at all, just tell me, and I'll try to do it for you."

"Well," said Tessie Bear, getting into Noddy's car, "I often wish we had a lamp-post outside our house. Every night my uncle bear bumps into the tree by our front gate, and when he goes 'Ouch!', it wakes us all up."

Noddy and Tessie drove off, leaving the Bunkey looking thoughtful.

That night the Bunkey crept into Noddy's front garden and whistled. Immediately the garage doors opened and out drove Noddy's car. The Bunkey climbed in and quickly drove out of the drive.

The next morning at breakfast the Bunkey kept
yawning.

"Are you tired?" Noddy asked.

"No," said the Bunkey. "I'm just practising opening
my mouth to put the boiled egg inside it."

Just then Mr Plod came in without knocking and marched straight up to Noddy.

"Noddy," he demanded, "do you know anything about four missing lamp-posts? One went from outside the Pink Cat's gate last night and one went from outside my gate – and we *both* heard the noise of a car . . ."

"Well, it wasn't my car!" said Noddy. "Please go away, Mr Plod."

"Yes, go away!" said the Bunkey, jumping up.

At that moment Tessie Bear came in. "There are four lamp-posts in our front garden! Wherever did . . . Oh, hello, Mr Plod."

"So that's where they have gone," said Mr Plod. "Noddy, you'll hear from me again!" he added darkly, as he left.

"Horrid fellow. I should have knocked his helmet off!" said the Bunkey.

"Bunkey," said Noddy sternly, "those lamp-posts, surely you didn't . . ."

"I must dash! I've got to weed the garden," said the Bunkey, rushing out of the door.

"He must have done it. Oh dear!" said Noddy, shaking his head.

Noddy and Tessie Bear followed
Bunkey into the garden and
found him frantically pulling up
weeds.

"Bunkey, you must tell the
truth," said Noddy.

"Look out, Noddy," Tessie Bear shouted. "Here comes Bumpy Dog! I'm afraid he'll be terribly pleased to see you!"

Bumpy Dog came running up and knocked Noddy over in his excitement to see him.

"Oh, do stop it, Bumpy Dog!" said Noddy, patting him.

But just then a weed came flying through the air and landed on Bumpy Dog's nose.

"Go away!" said Bunkey. "How dare you attack my friend."

He rushed at Bumpy Dog, but Bumpy Dog knocked him over.

Bunkey and Bumpy Dog chased each other all over Noddy's garden. At last, exhausted, they collapsed on to the garden seat, breaking it into bits.

"You stupid dog!" said Noddy crossly. "You've ruined my garden. And you are just as bad, Bunkey!"

"I'm sorry," said Bunkey. "I only wanted to protect you. I'll put your garden right again, I promise."

Later that day Noddy and Tessie returned to find that not only had the garden been replanted with new flowers, but the garden seat had been replaced.

"It's that Bunkey again!" cried Noddy. "That's not a garden seat, it's a park bench! Bunkey, come here!"

Bunkey crept out from behind the garden seat.

"I didn't steal them!" he pleaded. "I asked a park keeper whom the bench and the flowers belonged to. He said they belonged to everyone. That means they're yours, so I brought them home for you."

"Oh, you are silly, Bunkey, and such a nuisance!" said Noddy. "You had better come to the police station and own up about the lamp-posts and the park bench."

"No, I don't want to!" cried the Bunkey.

"Get in the car, Bunkey!" ordered Noddy.

At the police station Noddy pushed a reluctant Bunkey
in front of Mr Plod.

"Bunkey has come to say he's very sorry about taking
the lamp-posts and park bench . . ."

"Bunkey, indeed!" said Mr Plod, pulling off the Bunkey's hat. "There's no such thing. See, here are the ears sewn to the hat. He's a monkey, all right! I've just had a letter from the circus warning me about him. They'd had enough of his mischievous ways, so they threw him out of their caravan."

"You told me you had fallen out," said Noddy. "Oh, Bunkey, how could you . . ."

But Bunkey had already run outside and was climbing into Noddy's car.

"I'm sorry, Noddy," he called, as he drove off. "I only wanted to be your friend."

Noddy and Tessie trudged wearily home.

"I really miss my car. Will I ever see it again?" Noddy wondered sadly.

Just then they heard a "Parp! Parp!"

"My car!" cried Noddy. "Bunkey's sent it back!
Perhaps he was my friend after all."

"He only borrowed your car to get away because he
was frightened of Mr Plod," explained Tessie Bear.

"He really was a monkey, but I couldn't help liking him," Tessie Bear added.

"I liked him too," said Noddy. "He did always try to be kind, you know. I wonder whether he has found a new disguise!"

Laughing happily, Noddy and Tessie Bear went indoors, and neither of them even noticed the strange animal dancing on the garage roof, which was probably just as well.